For Louis
~ C W
For Nina, my god-daughter
~ A E

Text copyright © Catherine Walters 2009
Illustrations copyright © Alison Edgson 2009
Original edition published in English by Little Tiger Press,
an imprint of Magi Publications, London, England, 2009

Printed in China

Library of Congress Cataloging-in-Publication Data

Walters, Catherine, 1965-
The magical snowman / Catherine Walters ; illustrated by Alison Edgson.
p. cm.

Summary: Little Rabbit's father does not believe that Snowman is real, but when Little Rabbit
gets lost in swirling snow while gathering berries, the chilly friend he built comes to the rescue.
ISBN 978-1-56148-671-7 (hardcover : alk. paper)
[1. Snowmen--Fiction. 2. Magic--Fiction. 3. Rabbits--Fiction.
4. Fathers and sons--Fiction.] I. Edgson, Alison, ill. II. Title.

PZ7.W17127Mag 2009
[E]--dc22
2008055864

The Magical Snowman

Catherine Walters

Illustrated by Alison Edgson

Intercourse, PA 17534
800/762-7171
www.GoodBooks.com

It was a clear, sparkling winter's day. Little Rabbit had been busy all morning, heaping snow to make a snowman.

"Good work, Little Rabbit," said Daddy. "Could you finish it later though? I need you to find some berries for our tea."

"Snowman will be sad if I leave him now," Little Rabbit said.

"He'll be fine," said Daddy gently. "He's just a snowman. He isn't real."

"He *is* real!" said Little Rabbit.

"Of course he's real! He's my friend!"

Daddy smiled as he gave Little Rabbit a kiss. "Don't go too far," he said.

"I won't!" said Little Rabbit.

"Mmm, one for the basket and one for me," he sang as he skipped down the lane. Soon his paws were sticky with purple juice.

Little Rabbit was having so much fun . . .

he hardly noticed the snow beginning to fall.

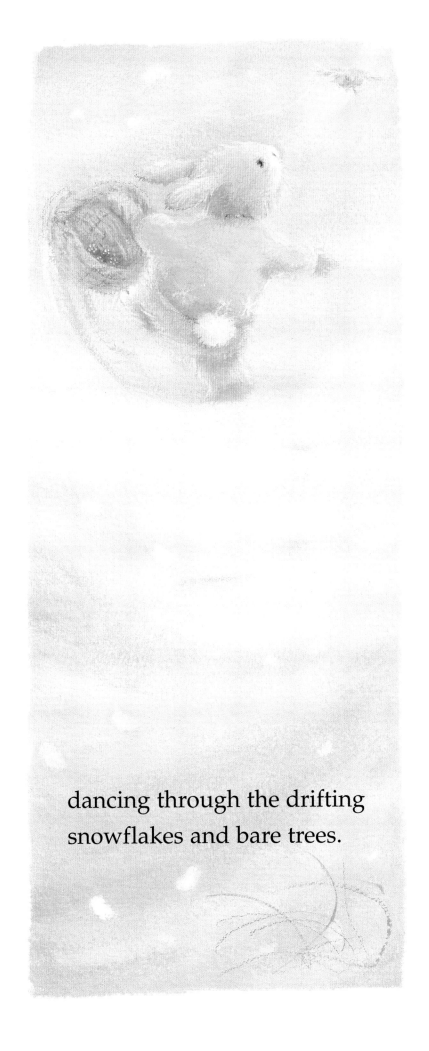

A robin flitted ahead of
him and he followed it . . .

dancing through the drifting
snowflakes and bare trees.

Then the robin flew away. Little Rabbit stopped and looked around. He wasn't sure which way he had come. The swirling snow made everything look strange.

"What will I do?" he cried. "How will I get home?"

As if in answer, a soft light sparkled through the trees. Smiling through the falling snow was his very own Snowman!

"I *knew* you were real!" said Little Rabbit.
"But, Snowman, I was all on my own."
 "Not all alone," smiled Snowman.
"I was there too, little friend. I was always
   there for you."

Snowman dusted flakes from Little Rabbit's fur and lifted him on to his shoulders.

"I'll take you home," he said. "Hold on tight!"

They whizzed down the hill . . .

WHOOOOOOOOOSH!

and landed in a snowy heap
by a frozen stream. WHUMPH!

"Here we go!" Snowman laughed as he held Little Rabbit's paw.

The world whisked by in a shimmer of silver frost. It felt as if they were flying.

"I'm coming home, Daddy!" Little Rabbit called.

WHEEEEEEEEEE!

Suddenly, Snowman skidded to a halt at the
bottom of a hill.

"We'll have to walk now," he said, as he
swung Little Rabbit into his soft arms.

"Are we nearly there yet?" yawned
Little Rabbit.

"Not far now," said Snowman.

Meanwhile, Daddy Rabbit was hurrying through the whirling snow. He was very worried and he shivered in the icy wind.

"Little Rabbit!" he called. "Little Rabbit! Where are you?"

"Daddy!" cried Little Rabbit, when
he heard his call. He leaped from
Snowman's arms and bounded up
the garden.

Daddy Rabbit swept him up
and hugged him tight, forgetting
all about the berries.
   "Thank goodness you're safe!"
he said. "I was so worried about
you, all alone."

"I wasn't alone," said Little Rabbit. "Snowman
took care of me."

"Oh did he now?" Daddy chuckled.

Snowman stood quietly in the winter darkness.
Little Rabbit smiled at him. And he saw Snowman
was smiling too.